W9-BYZ-458

MARVEL

AVENGERS
ULTRON REVOLUTION

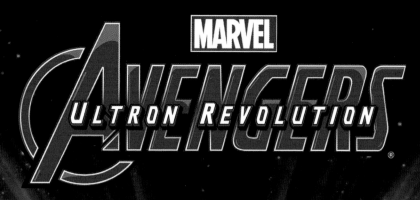

SAVING CAPTAIN ROGERS #3

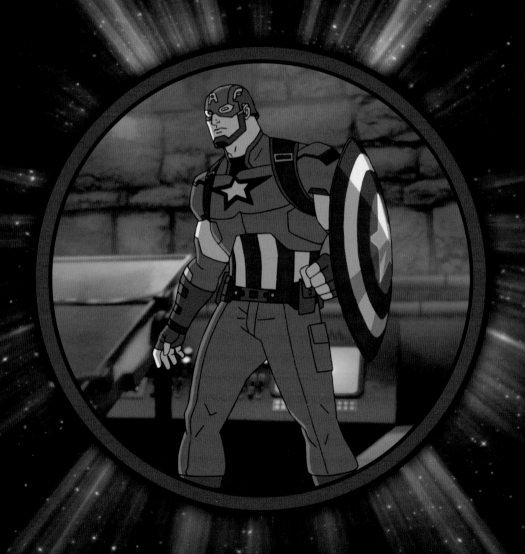

ABDO
Spotlight

ABDOBOOKS.COM

Reinforced library bound edition published in 2020 by Spotlight,
a division of ABDO, PO Box 398166, Minneapolis, Minnesota 55439.
Spotlight produces high-quality reinforced library bound editions for
schools and libraries. Published by agreement with Marvel Characters, Inc.

Printed in the United States of America, North Mankato, Minnesota.
042019
092019

THIS BOOK CONTAINS
RECYCLED MATERIALS

marvelkids.com

© 2020 MARVEL

Library of Congress Control Number: 2018965955

Publisher's Cataloging-in-Publication Data

Names: Caramagna, Joe; Scott, Mairghread, authors. | Marvel Animation Studios,
     illustrator.
Title: Saving captain Rogers / by Joe Caramagna ; Mairghread Scott; illustrated by
     Marvel Animation Studios.
Description: Minneapolis, Minnesota : Spotlight, 2020. | Series: Avengers: ultron
     revolution; #3
Summary: Iron Man and Black Widow head out to find a missing Cap, and track him
     down to a familiar castle in Europe where they find him hypnotized by Baron
     Helmut Zemo.
Identifiers: ISBN 9781532143489 (lib. bdg.)
Subjects: LCSH: Avengers (Fictitious characters)--Juvenile fiction. | Superheroes--
     Juvenile fiction. | Captain America (Fictitious character)--Juvenile fiction. |
     Graphic novels--Juvenile fiction. | Hypnosis--Juvenile fiction. | Kidnapping--
     Juvenile fiction. | Comic books, strips, etc--Juvenile fiction.
Classification: DDC 741.5--dc23

Spotlight

A Division of ABDO
abdobooks.com

In the closing months of WWII, Captain America and his partner Bucky were both presumed dead in an explosion over the English Channel.

Decades later, a figure was found trapped in ice, and Captain America was revived. Having slept through the majority of the 20th century, Steve Rogers awakened to a world he never imagined...a world in dire need of CAPTAIN AMERICA!

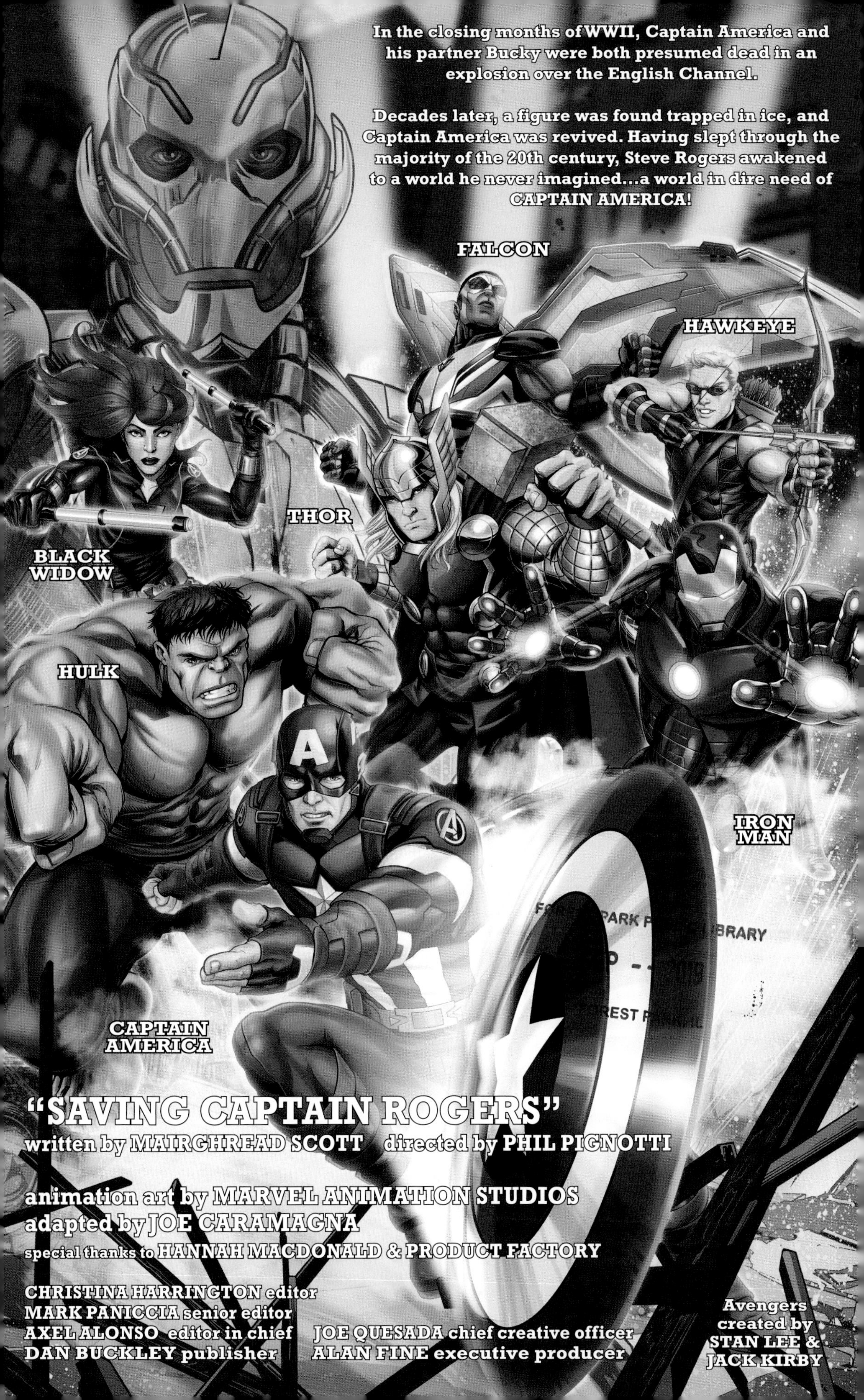

FALCON
HAWKEYE
THOR
BLACK WIDOW
HULK
IRON MAN
CAPTAIN AMERICA

"SAVING CAPTAIN ROGERS"

written by MAIRGHREAD SCOTT directed by PHIL PIGNOTTI

animation art by MARVEL ANIMATION STUDIOS
adapted by JOE CARAMAGNA
special thanks to HANNAH MACDONALD & PRODUCT FACTORY

CHRISTINA HARRINGTON editor
MARK PANICCIA senior editor
AXEL ALONSO editor in chief
DAN BUCKLEY publisher
JOE QUESADA chief creative officer
ALAN FINE executive producer

Avengers created by STAN LEE & JACK KIRBY

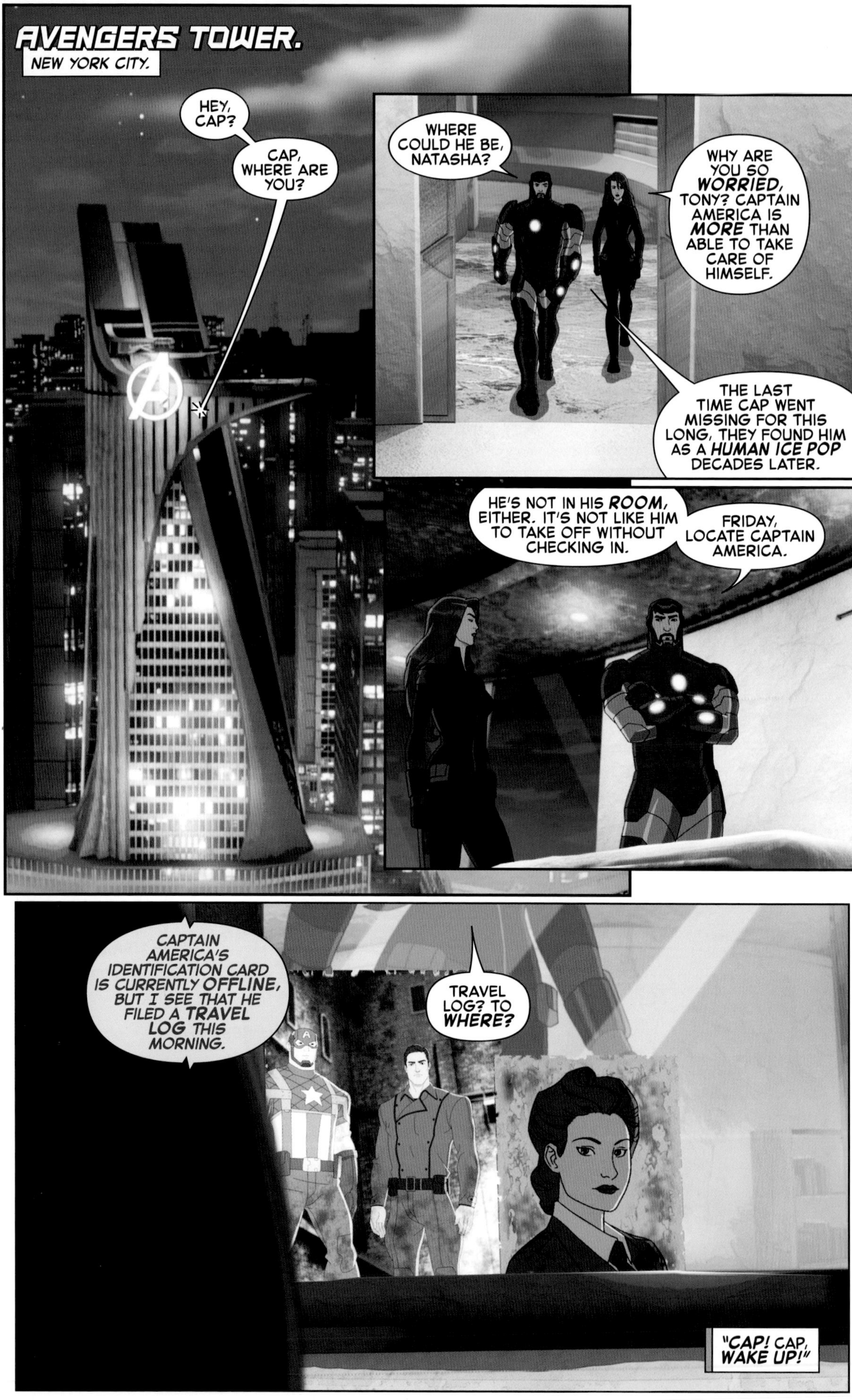
AVENGERS TOWER.
NEW YORK CITY.
HEY, CAP?
CAP, WHERE ARE YOU?
WHERE COULD HE BE, NATASHA?
WHY ARE YOU SO WORRIED, TONY? CAPTAIN AMERICA IS MORE THAN ABLE TO TAKE CARE OF HIMSELF.
THE LAST TIME CAP WENT MISSING FOR THIS LONG, THEY FOUND HIM AS A HUMAN ICE POP DECADES LATER.
HE'S NOT IN HIS ROOM, EITHER. IT'S NOT LIKE HIM TO TAKE OFF WITHOUT CHECKING IN.
FRIDAY, LOCATE CAPTAIN AMERICA.
CAPTAIN AMERICA'S IDENTIFICATION CARD IS CURRENTLY OFFLINE, BUT I SEE THAT HE FILED A TRAVEL LOG THIS MORNING.
TRAVEL LOG? TO WHERE?
"CAP! CAP, WAKE UP!"

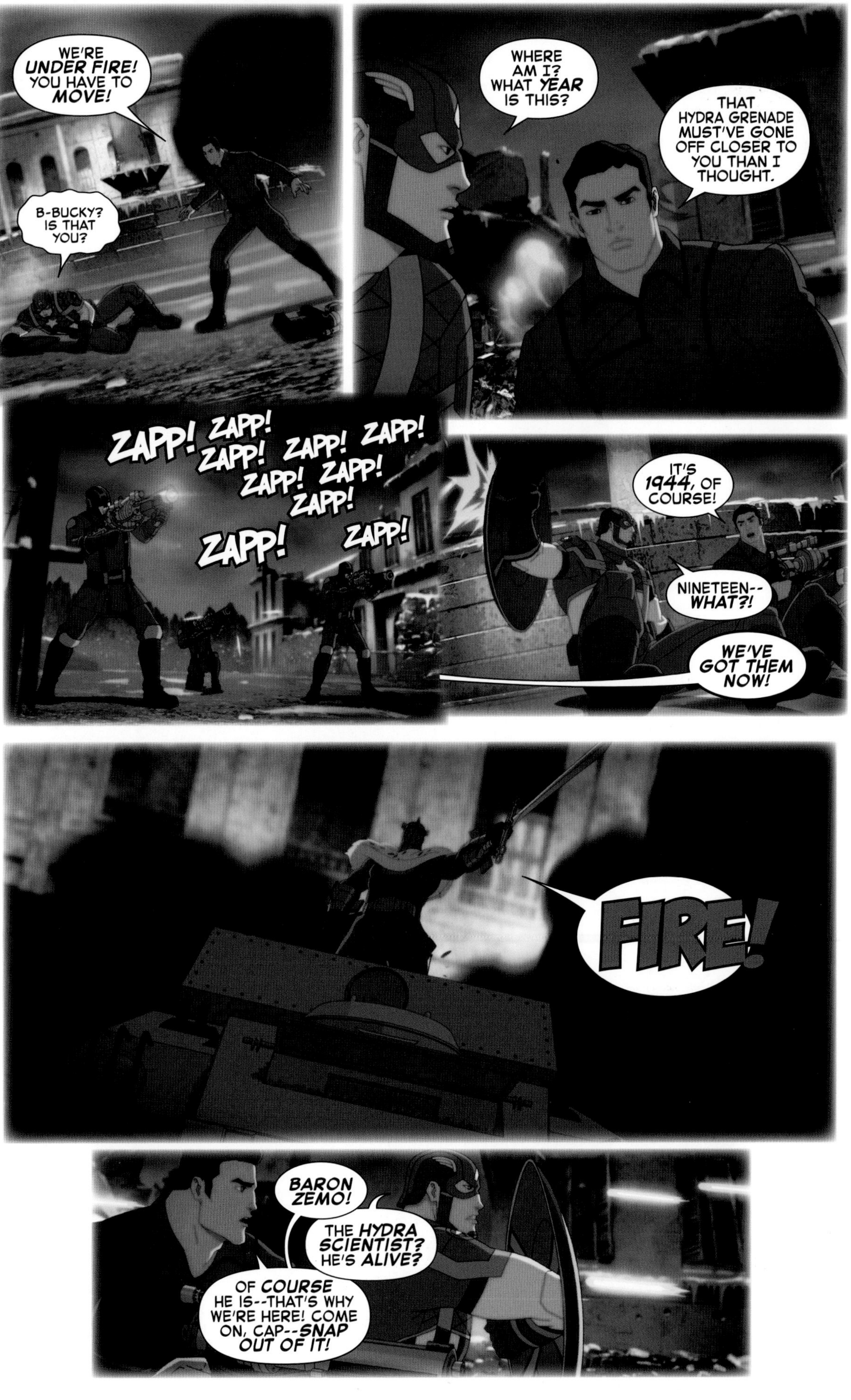
WE'RE UNDER FIRE! YOU HAVE TO MOVE!
B-BUCKY? IS THAT YOU?
WHERE AM I? WHAT YEAR IS THIS?
THAT HYDRA GRENADE MUST'VE GONE OFF CLOSER TO YOU THAN I THOUGHT.
ZAPP! ZAPP! ZAPP! ZAPP! ZAPP! ZAPP! ZAPP! ZAPP!
ZAPP! ZAPP!
IT'S 1944, OF COURSE!
NINETEEN--WHAT?!
WE'VE GOT THEM NOW!
FIRE!
BARON ZEMO!
THE HYDRA SCIENTIST? HE'S ALIVE?
OF COURSE HE IS--THAT'S WHY WE'RE HERE! COME ON, CAP--SNAP OUT OF IT!

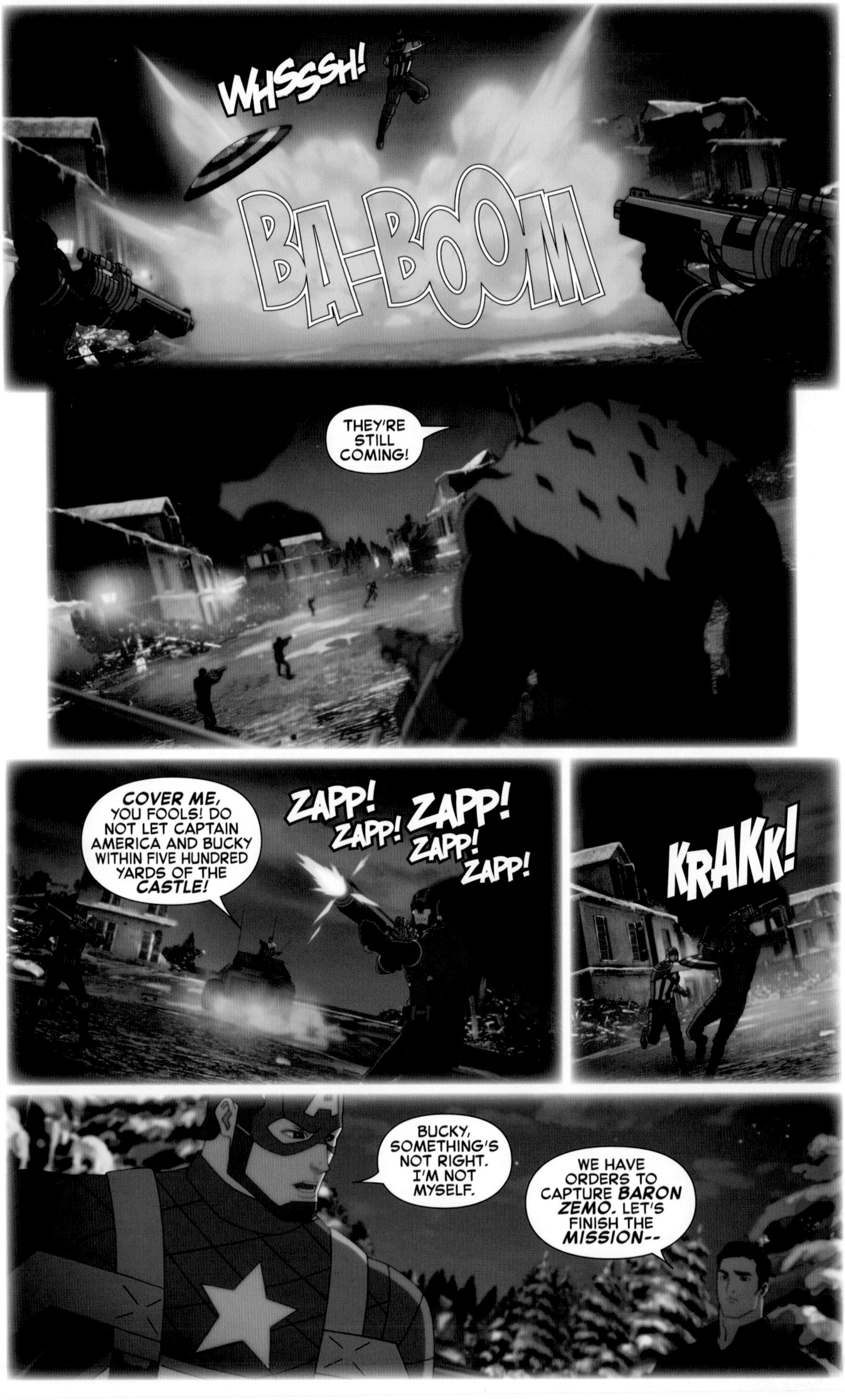
WHSSSH!
BA-BOOM
THEY'RE STILL COMING!
COVER ME, YOU FOOLS! DO NOT LET CAPTAIN AMERICA AND BUCKY WITHIN FIVE HUNDRED YARDS OF THE CASTLE!
ZAPP! ZAPP! ZAPP! ZAPP! ZAPP!
KRAKK!
BUCKY, SOMETHING'S NOT RIGHT. I'M NOT MYSELF.
WE HAVE ORDERS TO CAPTURE BARON ZEMO. LET'S FINISH THE MISSION--

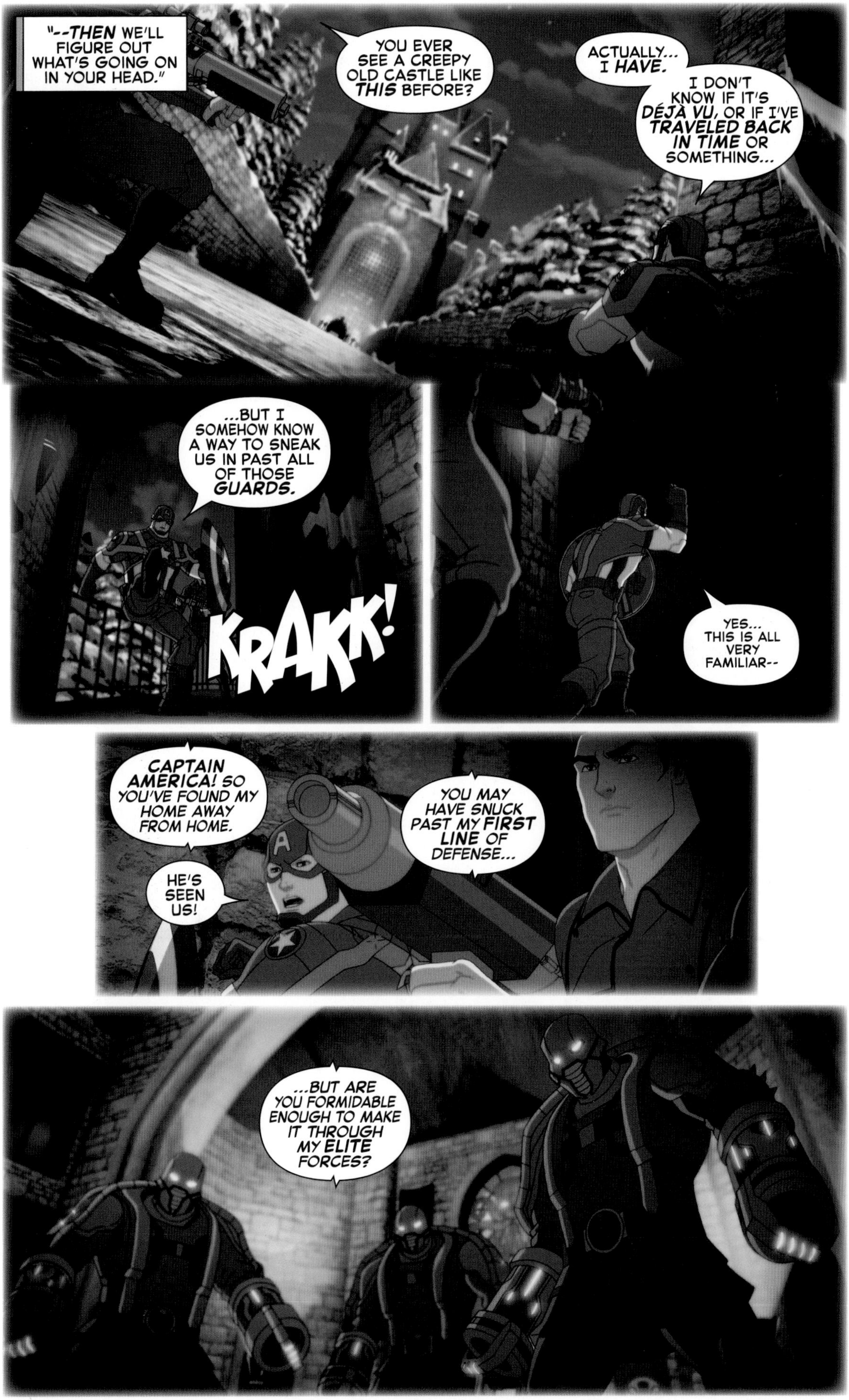
"--THEN WE'LL FIGURE OUT WHAT'S GOING ON IN YOUR HEAD."
YOU EVER SEE A CREEPY OLD CASTLE LIKE THIS BEFORE?
ACTUALLY... I HAVE.
I DON'T KNOW IF IT'S DÉJÀ VU, OR IF I'VE TRAVELED BACK IN TIME OR SOMETHING...
...BUT I SOMEHOW KNOW A WAY TO SNEAK US IN PAST ALL OF THOSE GUARDS.
KRAKK!
YES... THIS IS ALL VERY FAMILIAR--
CAPTAIN AMERICA! SO YOU'VE FOUND MY HOME AWAY FROM HOME.
HE'S SEEN US!
YOU MAY HAVE SNUCK PAST MY FIRST LINE OF DEFENSE...
...BUT ARE YOU FORMIDABLE ENOUGH TO MAKE IT THROUGH MY ELITE FORCES?

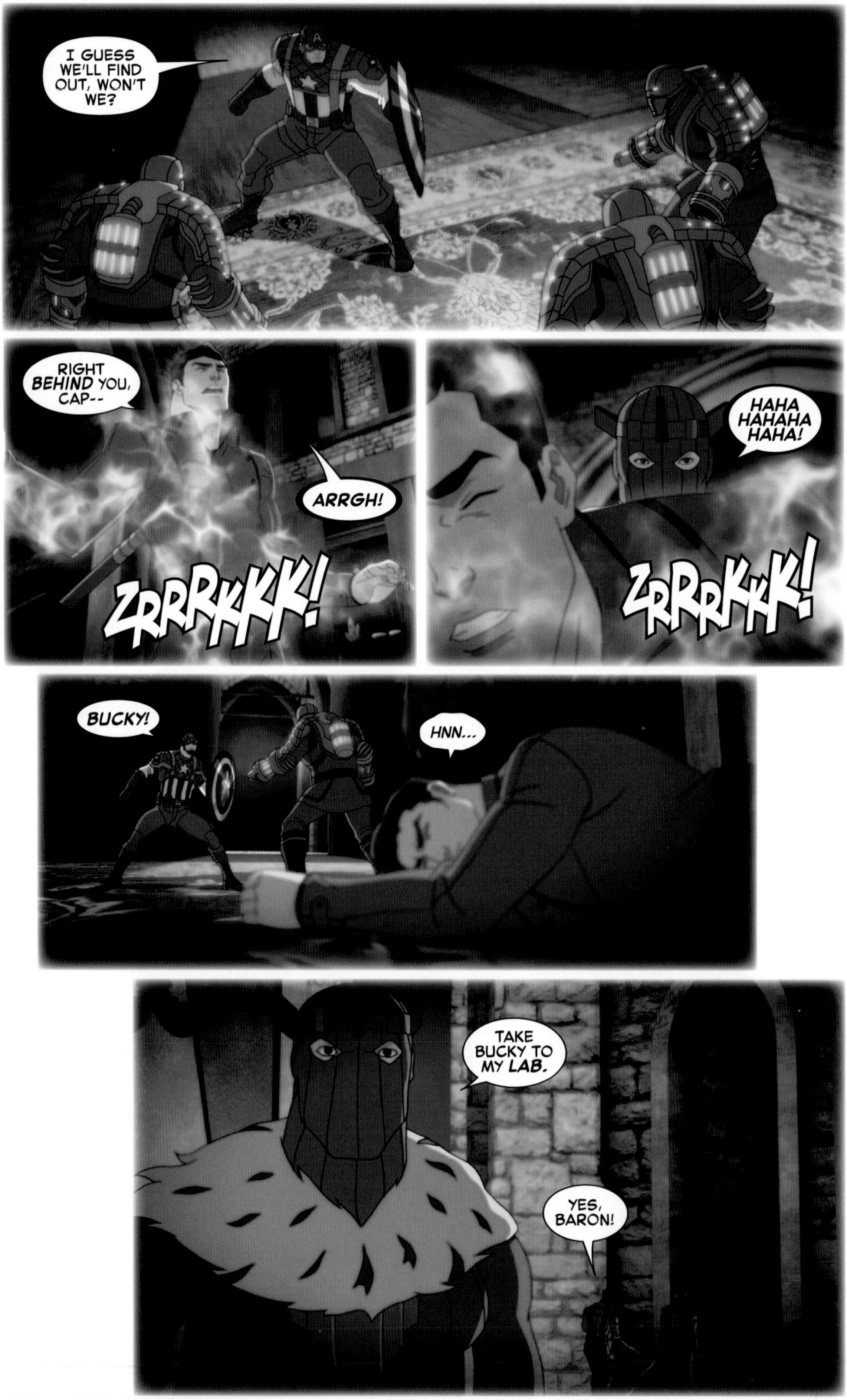
I GUESS WE'LL FIND OUT, WON'T WE?
RIGHT BEHIND YOU, CAP--
ARRGH!
ZRRRKKK!
HAHA HAHAHA HAHA!
ZRRRKKK!
BUCKY!
HNN...
TAKE BUCKY TO MY LAB.
YES, BARON!

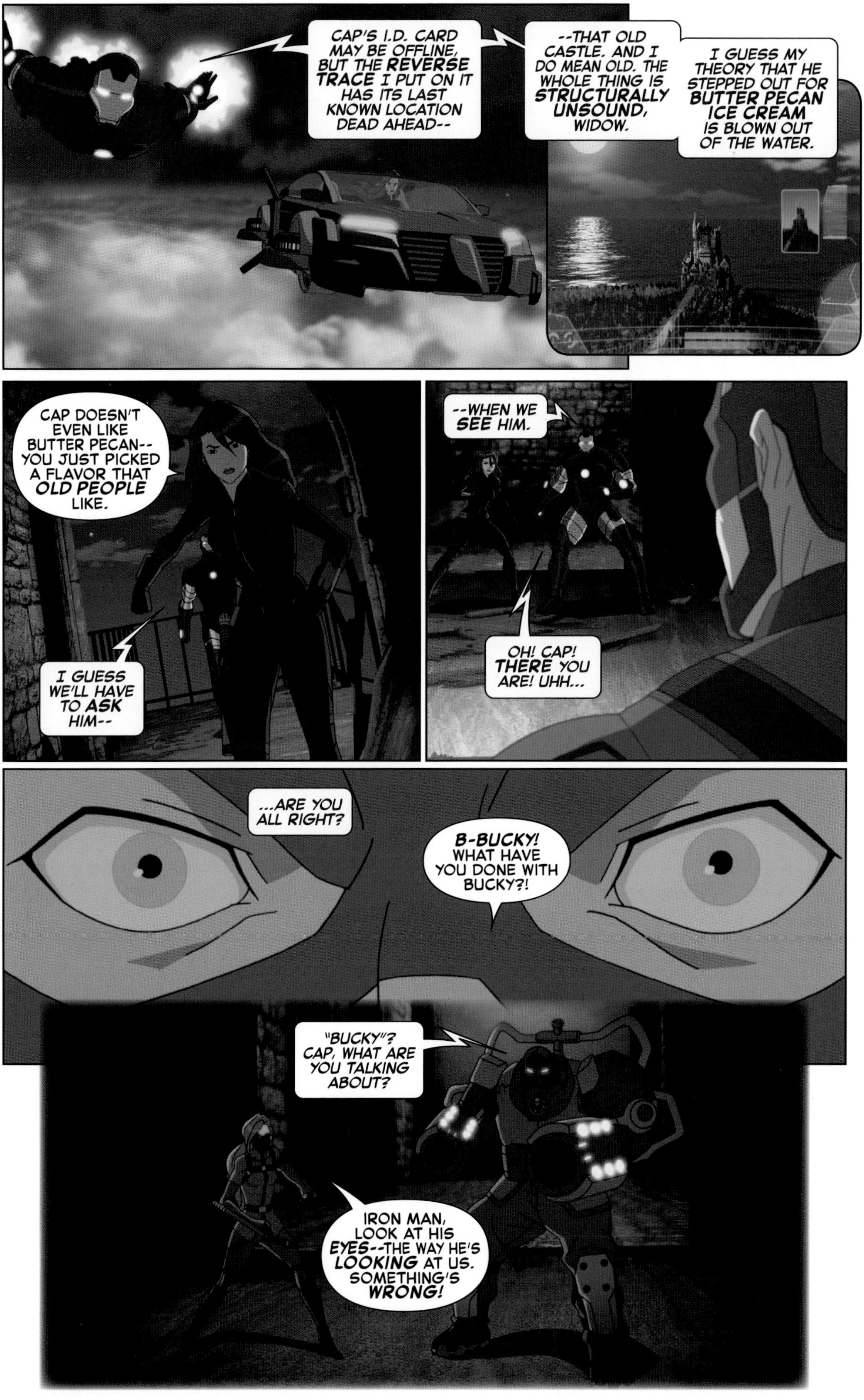
CAP'S I.D. CARD MAY BE OFFLINE, BUT THE REVERSE TRACE I PUT ON IT HAS ITS LAST KNOWN LOCATION DEAD AHEAD--
--THAT OLD CASTLE. AND I DO MEAN OLD. THE WHOLE THING IS STRUCTURALLY UNSOUND, WIDOW.
I GUESS MY THEORY THAT HE STEPPED OUT FOR BUTTER PECAN ICE CREAM IS BLOWN OUT OF THE WATER.
CAP DOESN'T EVEN LIKE BUTTER PECAN-- YOU JUST PICKED A FLAVOR THAT OLD PEOPLE LIKE.
I GUESS WE'LL HAVE TO ASK HIM--
--WHEN WE SEE HIM.
OH! CAP! THERE YOU ARE! UHH...
...ARE YOU ALL RIGHT?
B-BUCKY! WHAT HAVE YOU DONE WITH BUCKY?!
"BUCKY"? CAP, WHAT ARE YOU TALKING ABOUT?
IRON MAN, LOOK AT HIS EYES--THE WAY HE'S LOOKING AT US. SOMETHING'S WRONG!

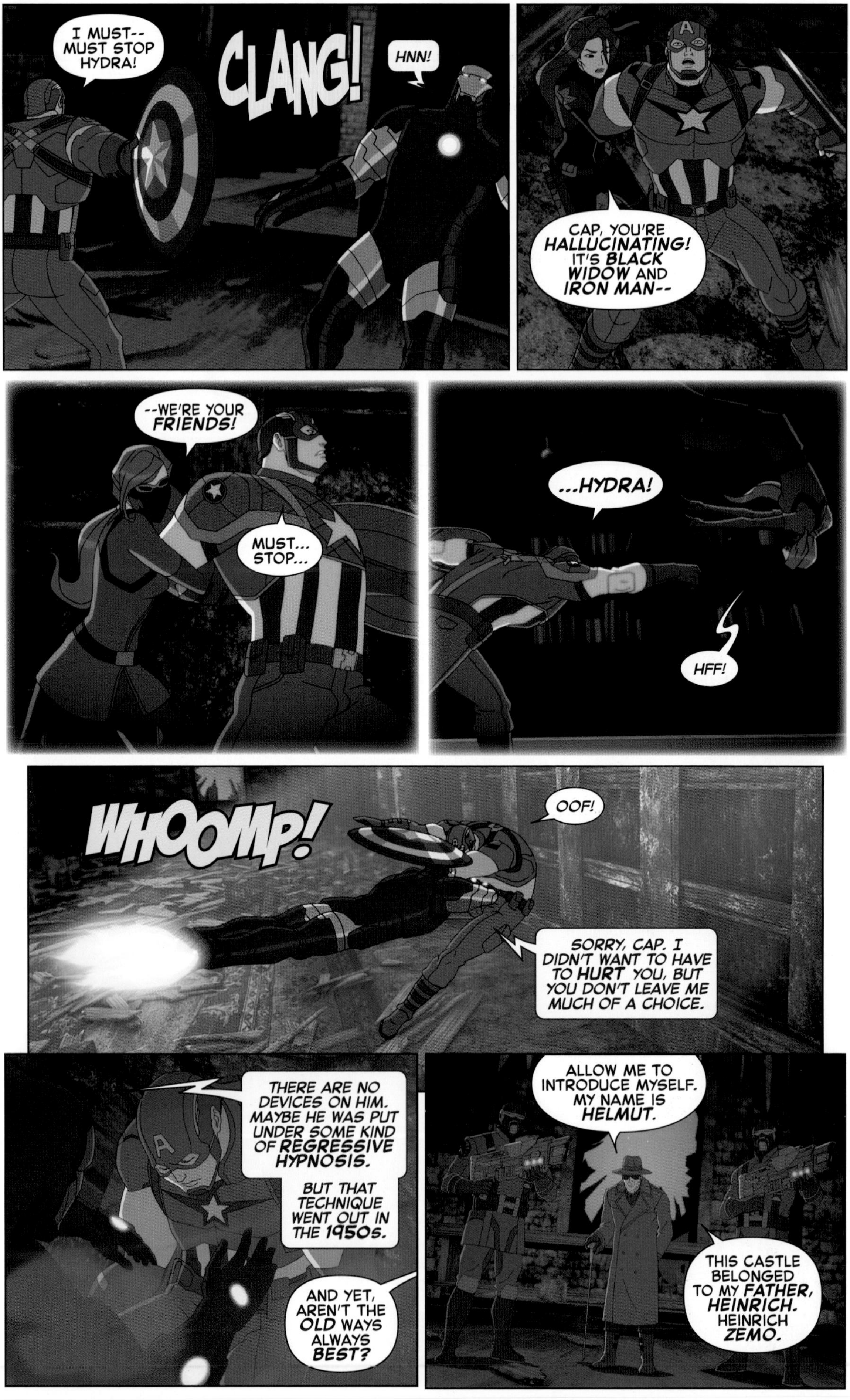
I MUST-- MUST STOP HYDRA!
CLANG!
HNN!
CAP, YOU'RE HALLUCINATING! IT'S BLACK WIDOW AND IRON MAN--
--WE'RE YOUR FRIENDS!
MUST... STOP...
...HYDRA!
HFF!
WHOOMP!
OOF!
SORRY, CAP. I DIDN'T WANT TO HAVE TO HURT YOU, BUT YOU DON'T LEAVE ME MUCH OF A CHOICE.
THERE ARE NO DEVICES ON HIM. MAYBE HE WAS PUT UNDER SOME KIND OF REGRESSIVE HYPNOSIS.
BUT THAT TECHNIQUE WENT OUT IN THE 1950s.
AND YET, AREN'T THE OLD WAYS ALWAYS BEST?
ALLOW ME TO INTRODUCE MYSELF. MY NAME IS HELMUT.
THIS CASTLE BELONGED TO MY FATHER, HEINRICH. HEINRICH ZEMO.

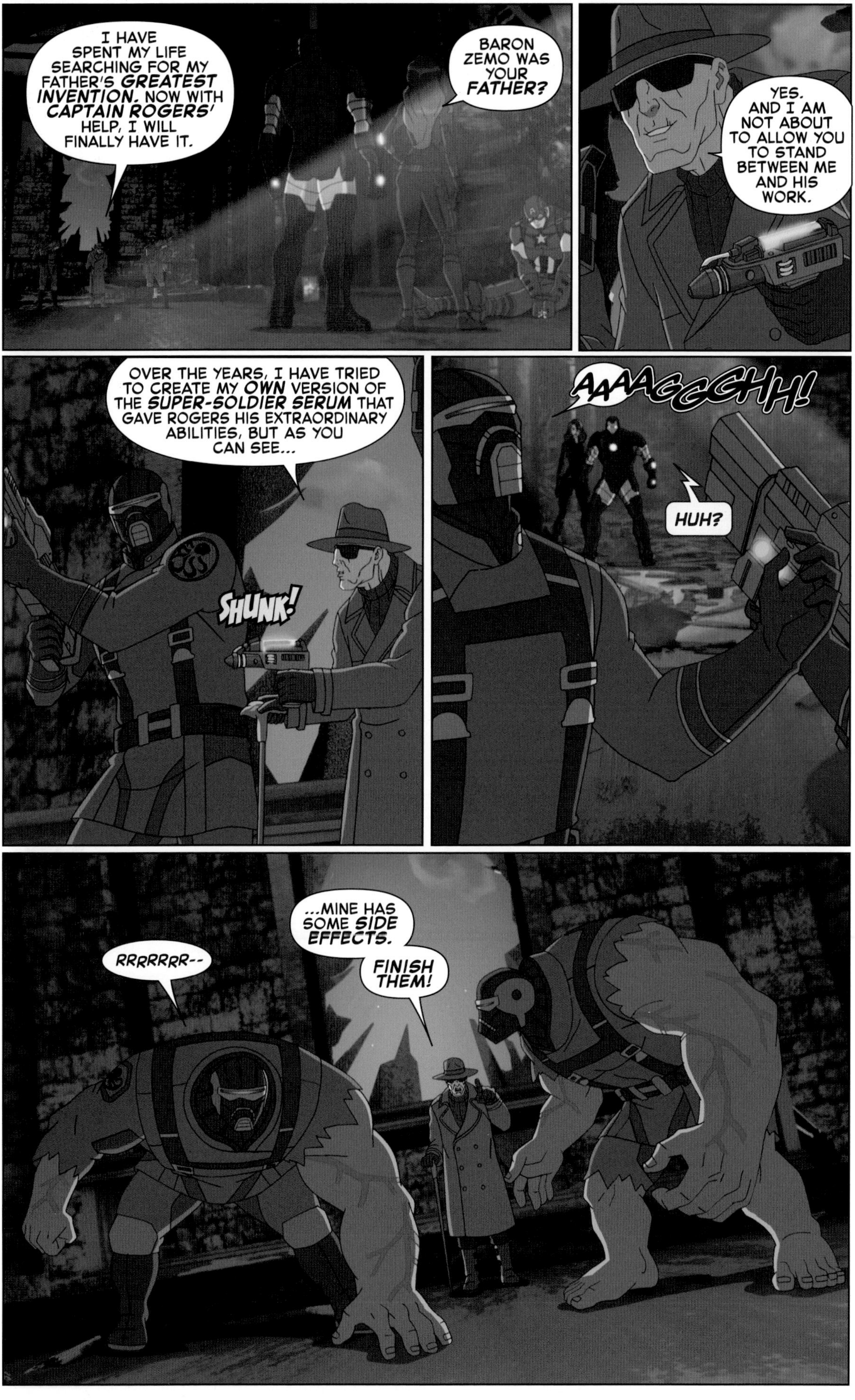
I HAVE SPENT MY LIFE SEARCHING FOR MY FATHER'S GREATEST INVENTION. NOW WITH CAPTAIN ROGERS' HELP, I WILL FINALLY HAVE IT.
BARON ZEMO WAS YOUR FATHER?
YES. AND I AM NOT ABOUT TO ALLOW YOU TO STAND BETWEEN ME AND HIS WORK.
OVER THE YEARS, I HAVE TRIED TO CREATE MY OWN VERSION OF THE SUPER-SOLDIER SERUM THAT GAVE ROGERS HIS EXTRAORDINARY ABILITIES, BUT AS YOU CAN SEE...
SHUNK!
AAAAGGGHH!
HUH?
...MINE HAS SOME SIDE EFFECTS.
FINISH THEM!
RRRRRRR--

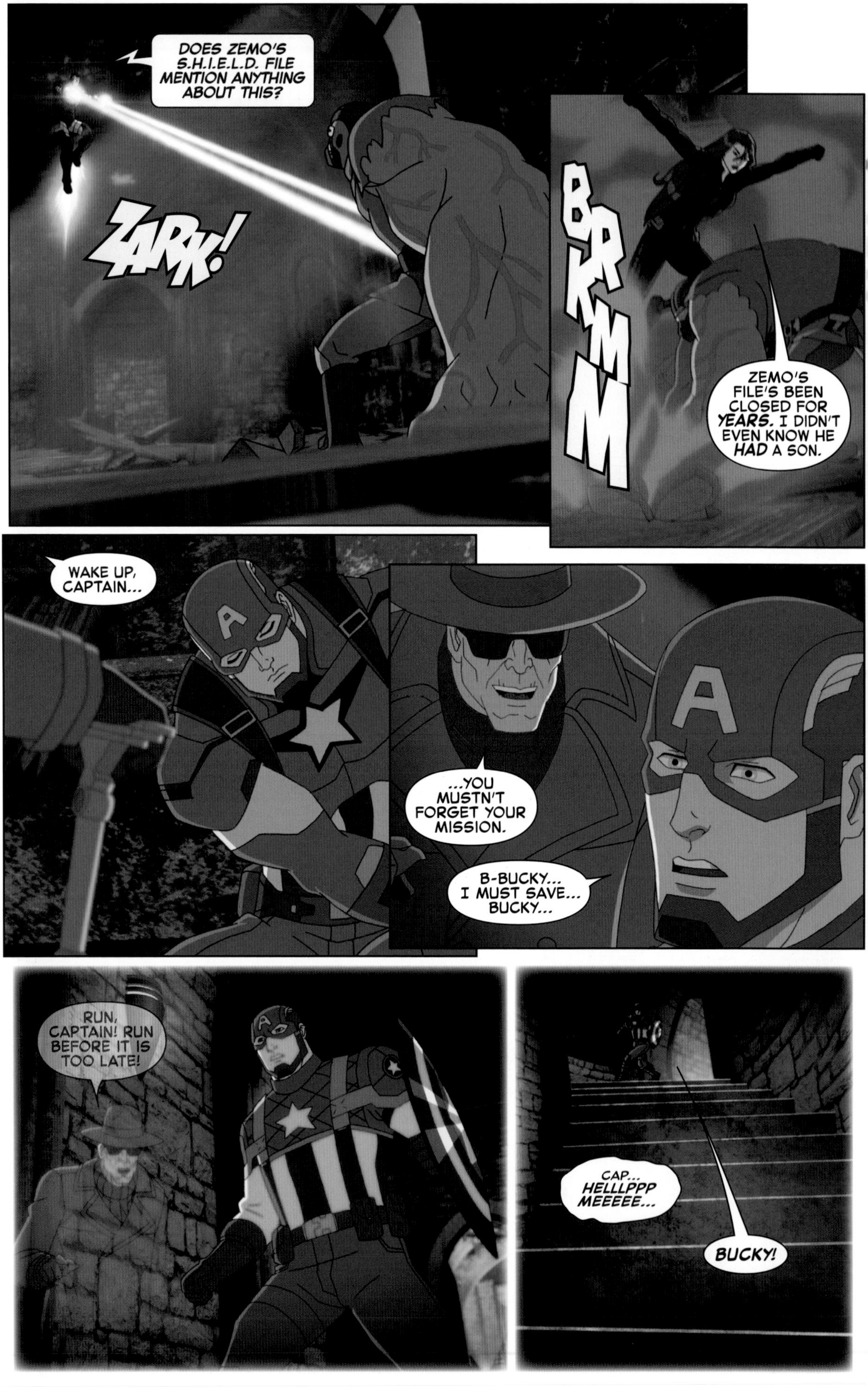
DOES ZEMO'S S.H.I.E.L.D. FILE MENTION ANYTHING ABOUT THIS?
ZARK!
BRKMM
ZEMO'S FILE'S BEEN CLOSED FOR YEARS. I DIDN'T EVEN KNOW HE HAD A SON.
WAKE UP, CAPTAIN...
...YOU MUSTN'T FORGET YOUR MISSION.
B-BUCKY... I MUST SAVE... BUCKY...
RUN, CAPTAIN! RUN BEFORE IT IS TOO LATE!
CAP... HELLLPPP MEEEEE...
BUCKY!

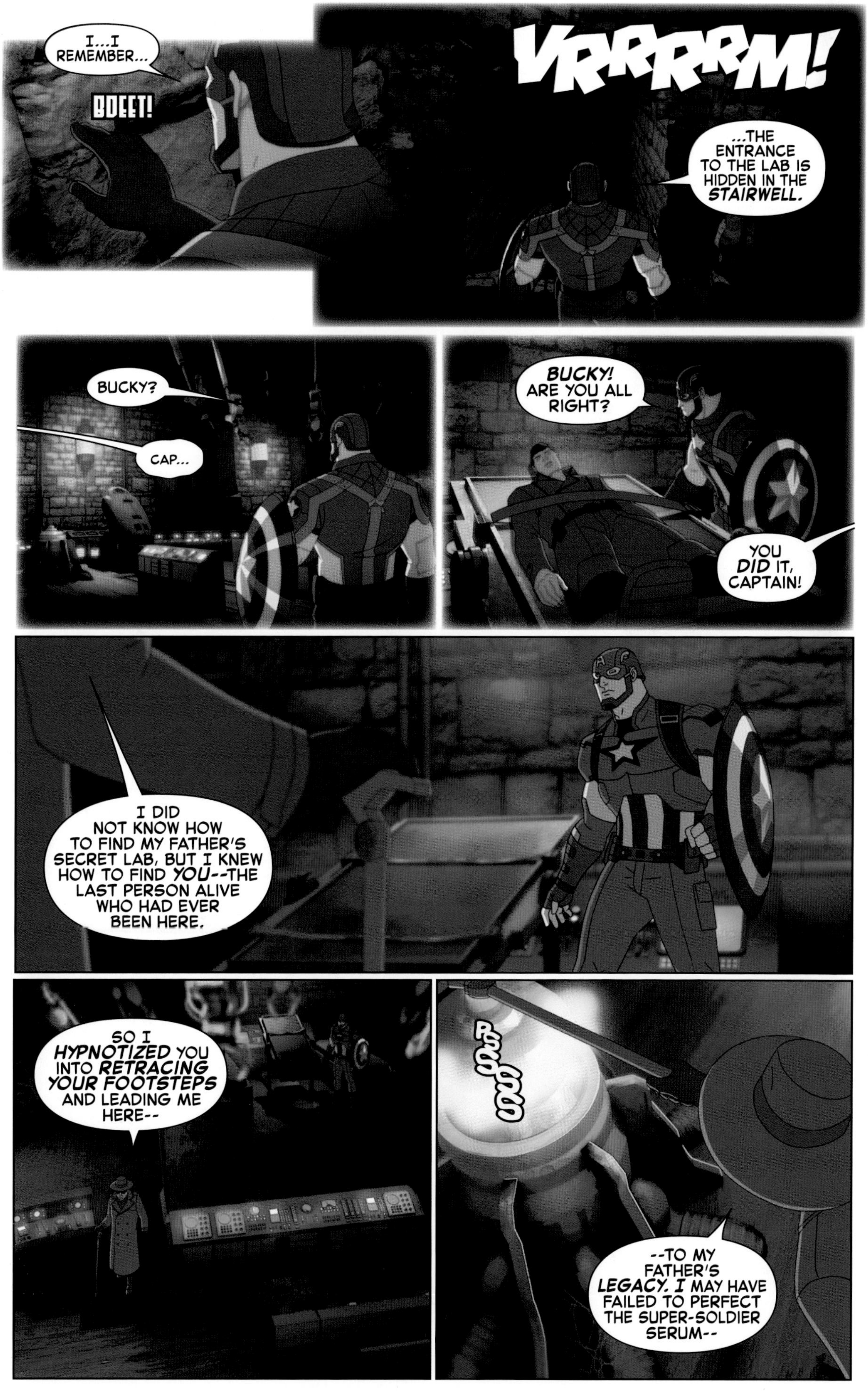

I...I REMEMBER...
BDEET!
VRRRRM!
...THE ENTRANCE TO THE LAB IS HIDDEN IN THE *STAIRWELL.*
BUCKY?
CAP...
BUCKY! ARE YOU ALL RIGHT?
YOU *DID* IT, CAPTAIN!
I DID NOT KNOW HOW TO FIND MY FATHER'S SECRET LAB, BUT I KNEW HOW TO FIND *YOU*--THE LAST PERSON ALIVE WHO HAD EVER BEEN HERE.
SO I *HYPNOTIZED* YOU INTO *RETRACING YOUR FOOTSTEPS* AND LEADING ME HERE--
--TO MY FATHER'S *LEGACY. I* MAY HAVE FAILED TO PERFECT THE SUPER-SOLDIER SERUM--

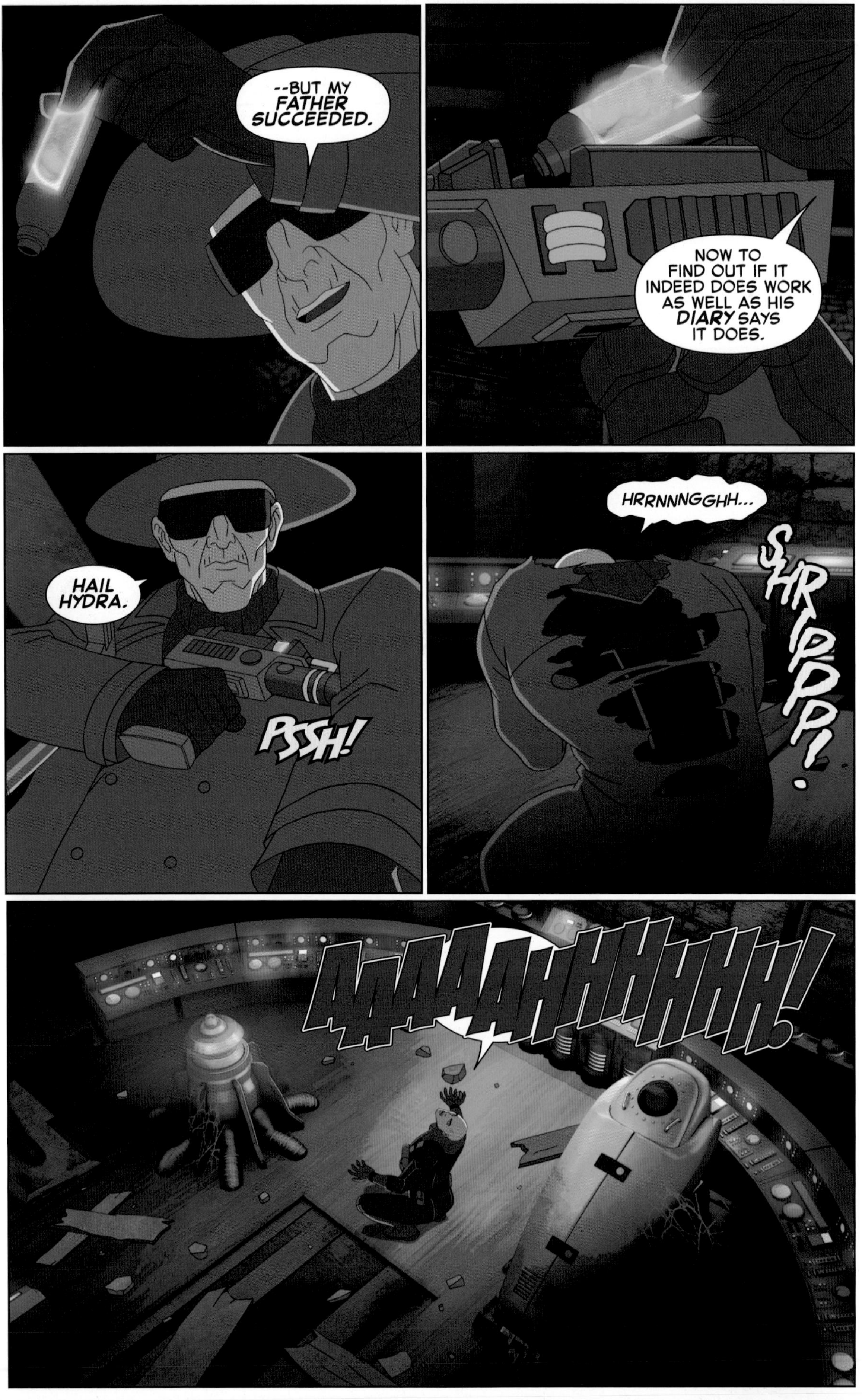
--BUT MY FATHER SUCCEEDED.
NOW TO FIND OUT IF IT INDEED DOES WORK AS WELL AS HIS DIARY SAYS IT DOES.
HAIL HYDRA.
PSSH!
HRRNNNGGHH...
SHRIPPP!
AAAAAHHHHHHH!

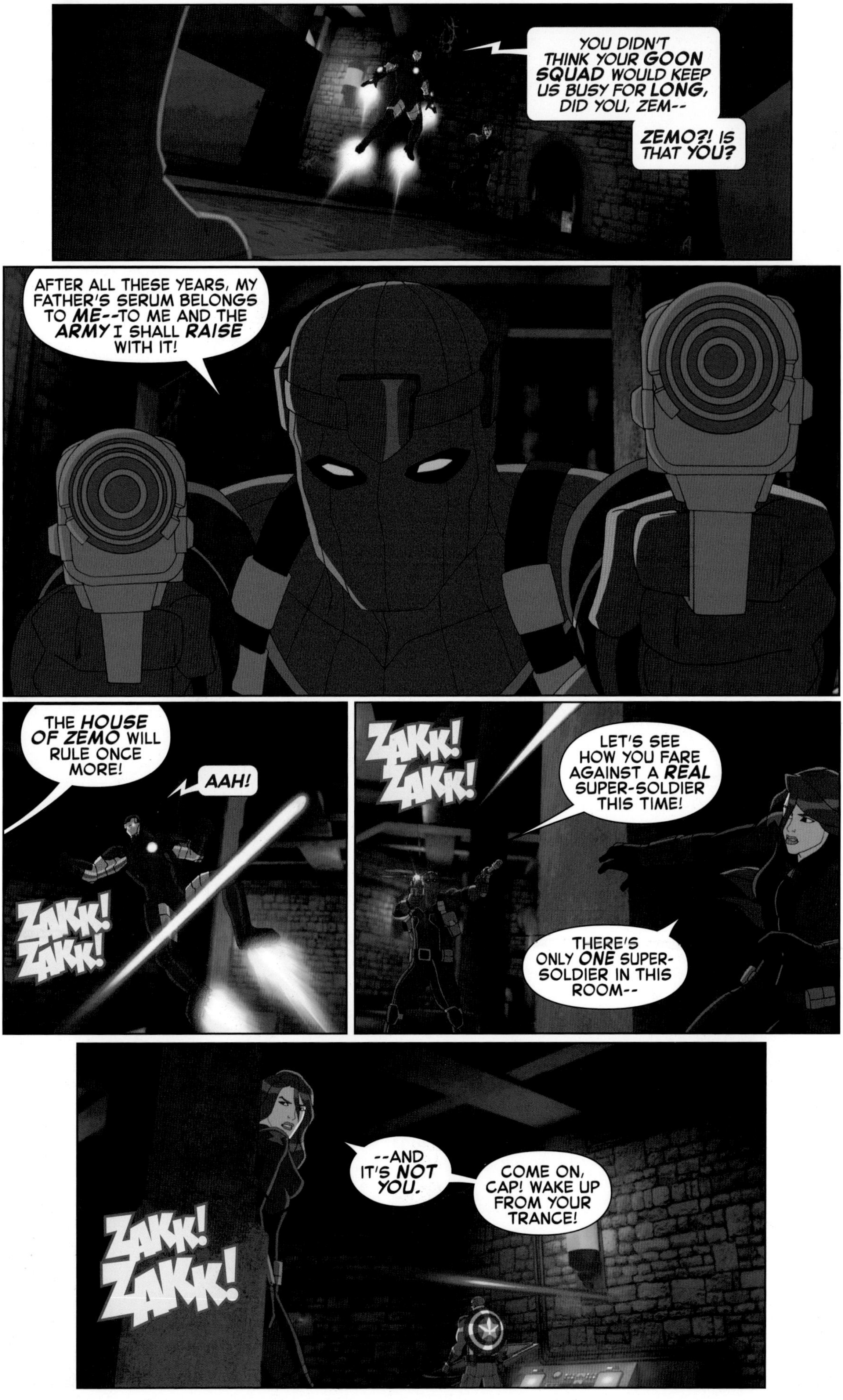

YOU DIDN'T THINK YOUR GOON SQUAD WOULD KEEP US BUSY FOR LONG, DID YOU, ZEM--
ZEMO?! IS THAT YOU?
AFTER ALL THESE YEARS, MY FATHER'S SERUM BELONGS TO ME--TO ME AND THE ARMY I SHALL RAISE WITH IT!
THE HOUSE OF ZEMO WILL RULE ONCE MORE!
AAH!
ZAKK! ZAKK!
ZAKK! ZAKK!
LET'S SEE HOW YOU FARE AGAINST A REAL SUPER-SOLDIER THIS TIME!
THERE'S ONLY ONE SUPER-SOLDIER IN THIS ROOM--
--AND IT'S NOT YOU.
COME ON, CAP! WAKE UP FROM YOUR TRANCE!
ZAKK! ZAKK!

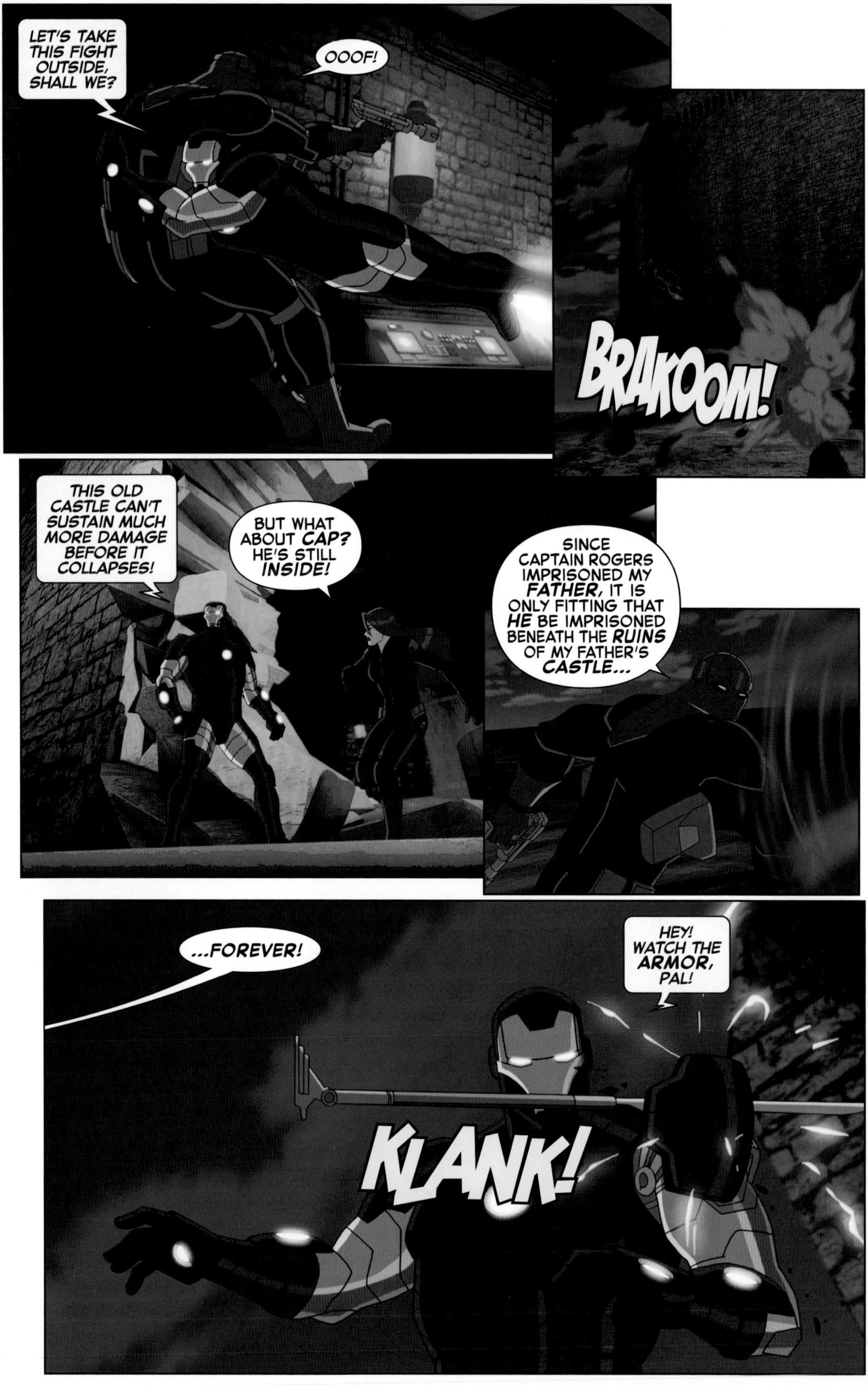

LET'S TAKE THIS FIGHT OUTSIDE, SHALL WE?
OOOF!
BRAKOOM!
THIS OLD CASTLE CAN'T SUSTAIN MUCH MORE DAMAGE BEFORE IT COLLAPSES!
BUT WHAT ABOUT CAP? HE'S STILL INSIDE!
SINCE CAPTAIN ROGERS IMPRISONED MY FATHER, IT IS ONLY FITTING THAT HE BE IMPRISONED BENEATH THE RUINS OF MY FATHER'S CASTLE...
...FOREVER!
HEY! WATCH THE ARMOR, PAL!
KLANK!

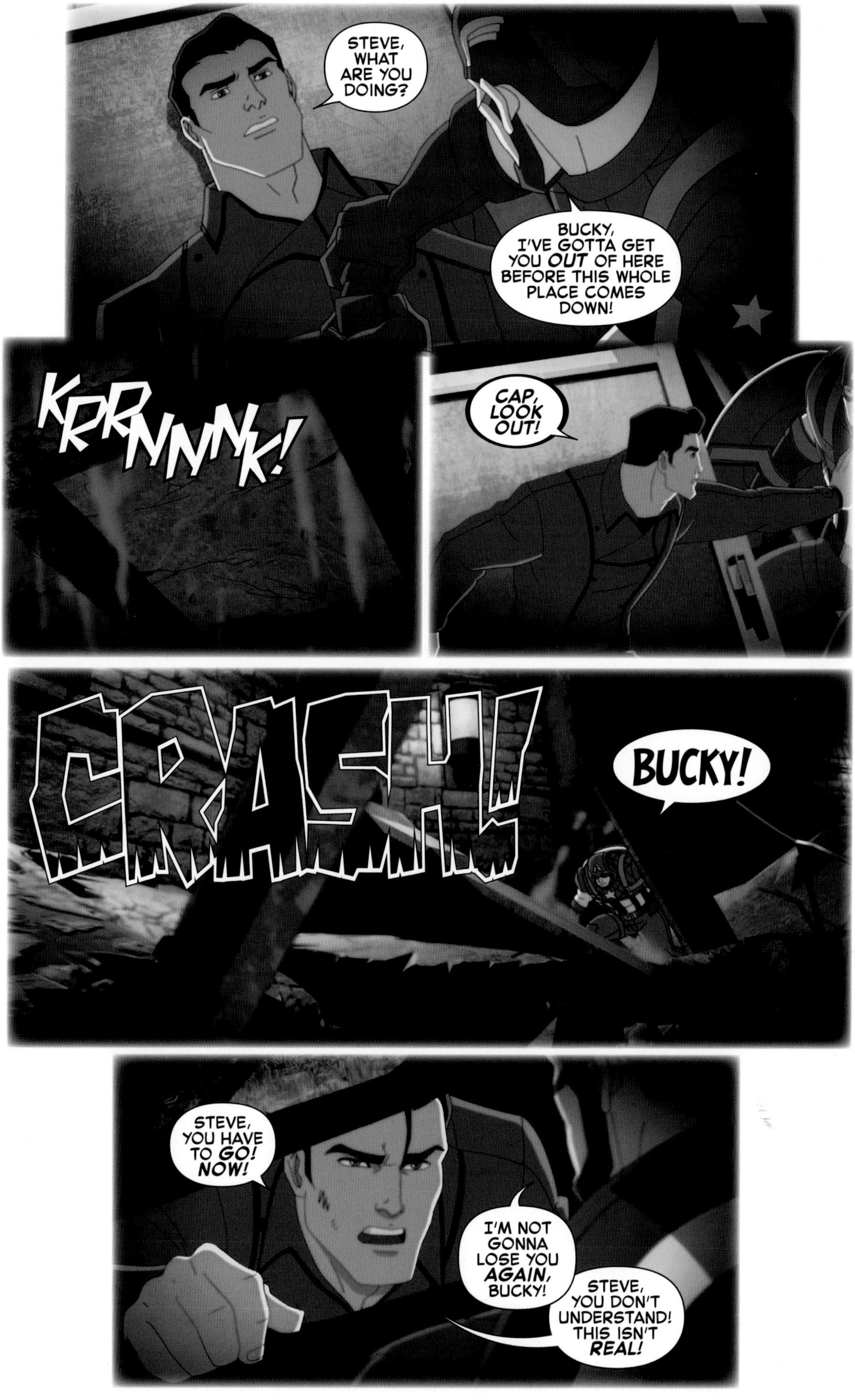
STEVE, WHAT ARE YOU DOING?
BUCKY, I'VE GOTTA GET YOU OUT OF HERE BEFORE THIS WHOLE PLACE COMES DOWN!
KRRNNNK!
CAP, LOOK OUT!
CRASH!
BUCKY!
STEVE, YOU HAVE TO GO! NOW!
I'M NOT GONNA LOSE YOU AGAIN, BUCKY!
STEVE, YOU DON'T UNDERSTAND! THIS ISN'T REAL!

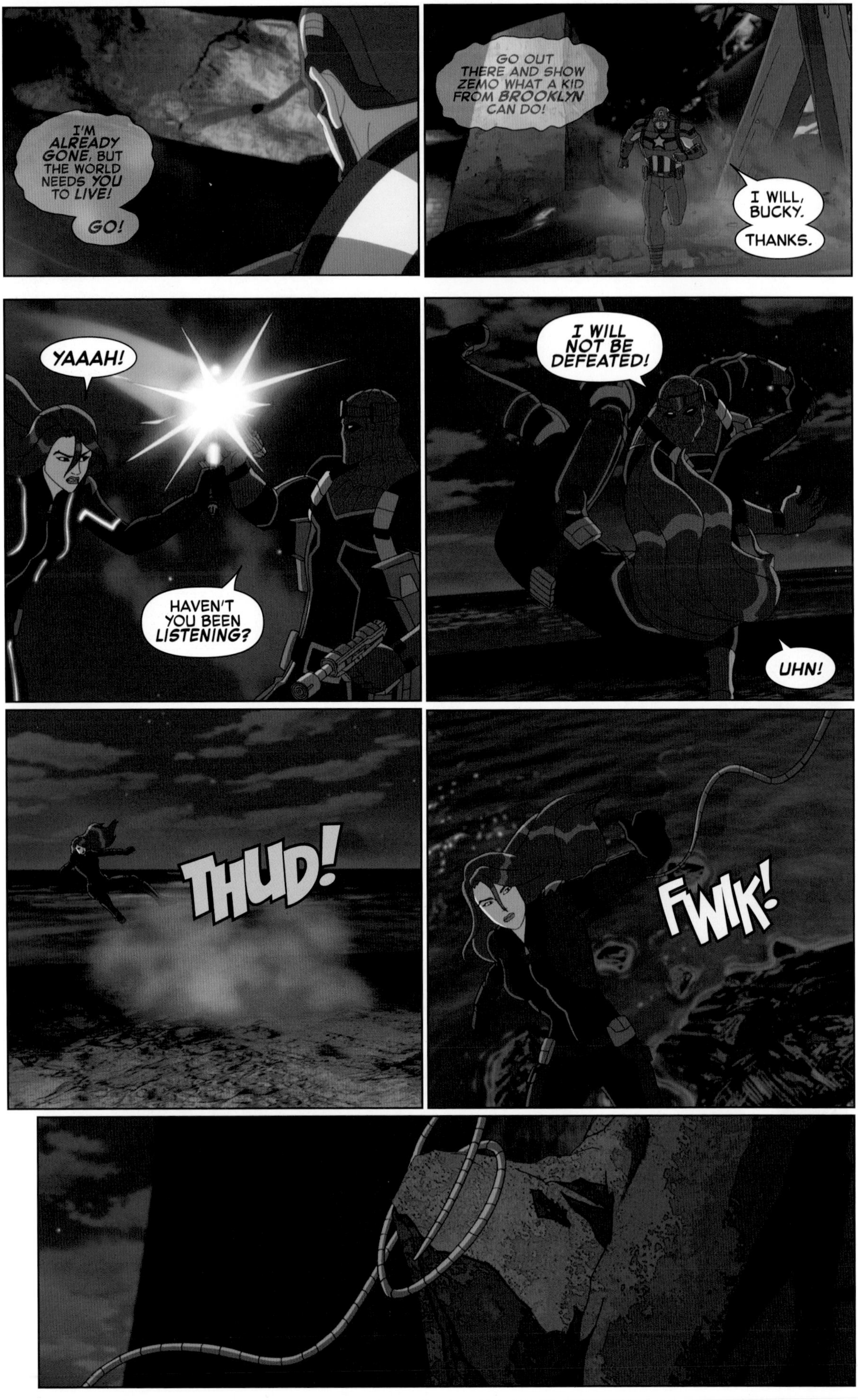
I'M ALREADY GONE, BUT THE WORLD NEEDS YOU TO LIVE!
GO!
GO OUT THERE AND SHOW ZEMO WHAT A KID FROM BROOKLYN CAN DO!
I WILL, BUCKY.
THANKS.
YAAAH!
HAVEN'T YOU BEEN LISTENING?
I WILL NOT BE DEFEATED!
UHN!
THUD!
FWIK!

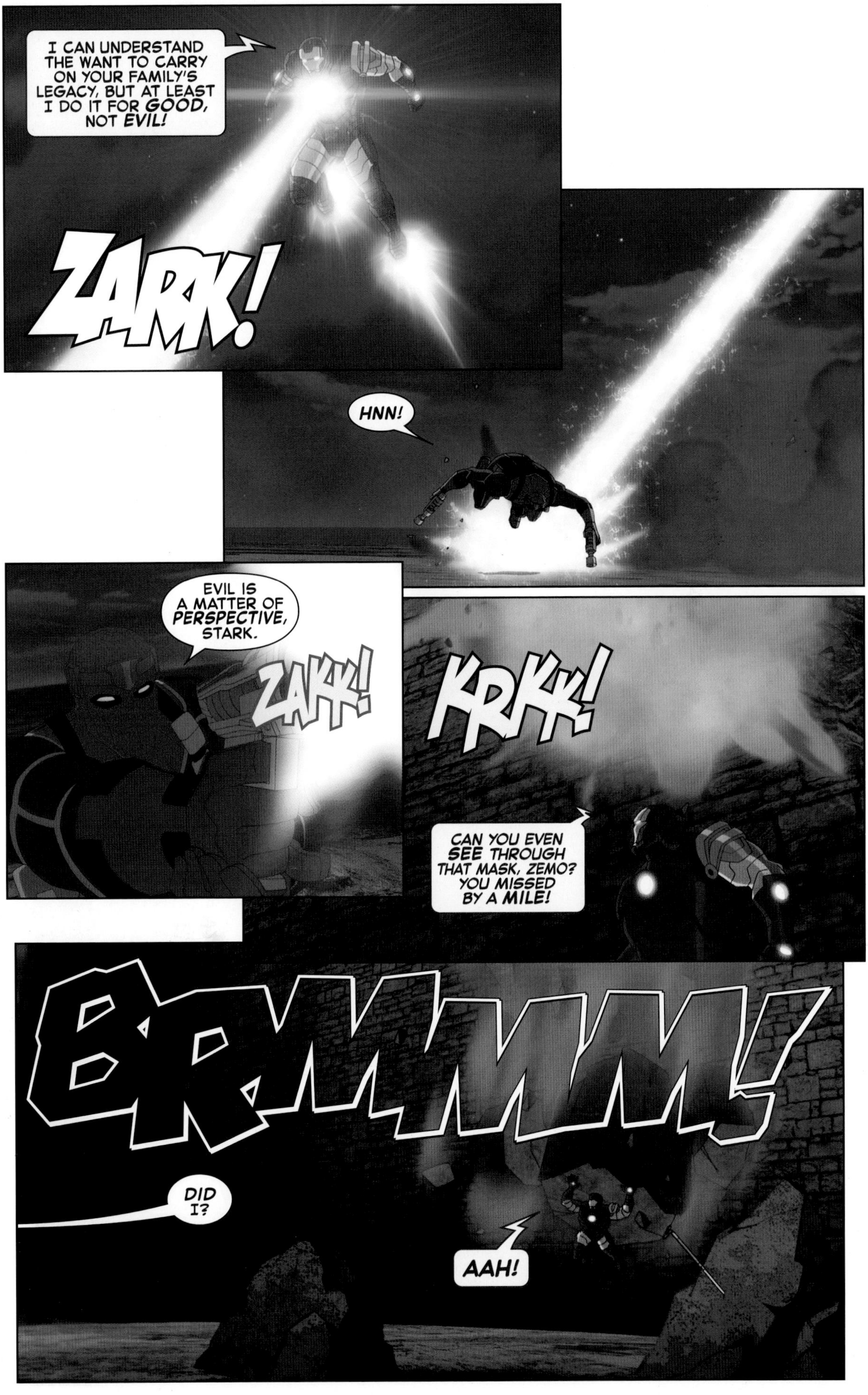
I CAN UNDERSTAND THE WANT TO CARRY ON YOUR FAMILY'S LEGACY, BUT AT LEAST I DO IT FOR GOOD, NOT EVIL!
ZARK!
HNN!
EVIL IS A MATTER OF PERSPECTIVE, STARK.
ZAKK!
KRKK!
CAN YOU EVEN SEE THROUGH THAT MASK, ZEMO? YOU MISSED BY A MILE!
BRMMM!
DID I?
AAH!

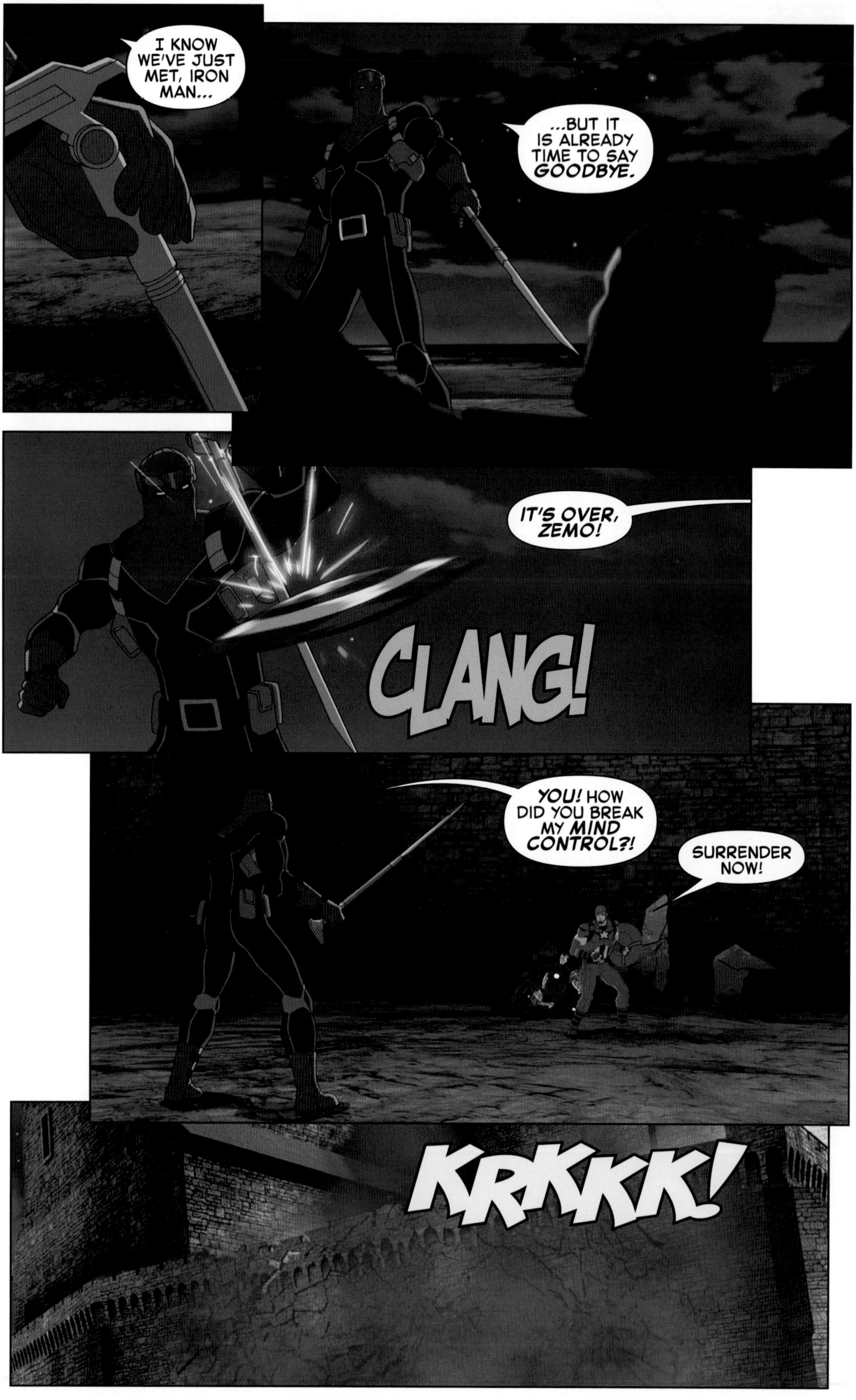
I KNOW WE'VE JUST MET, IRON MAN...
...BUT IT IS ALREADY TIME TO SAY GOODBYE.
IT'S OVER, ZEMO!
CLANG!
YOU! HOW DID YOU BREAK MY MIND CONTROL?!
SURRENDER NOW!
KRKKK!

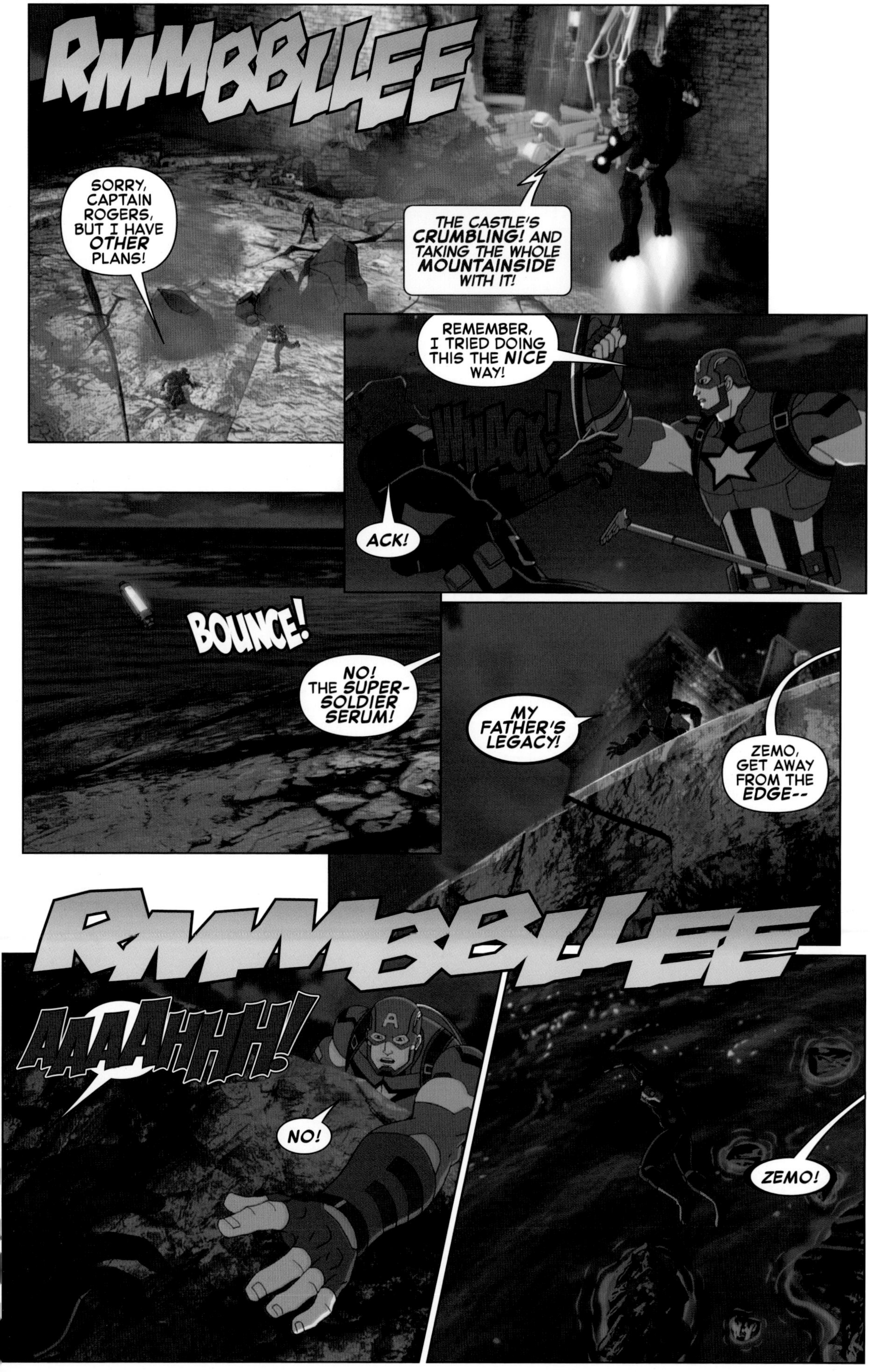
RMMBBLLEE
SORRY, CAPTAIN ROGERS, BUT I HAVE OTHER PLANS!
THE CASTLE'S CRUMBLING! AND TAKING THE WHOLE MOUNTAINSIDE WITH IT!
REMEMBER, I TRIED DOING THIS THE NICE WAY!
WHHACK!
ACK!
BOUNCE!
NO! THE SUPER-SOLDIER SERUM!
MY FATHER'S LEGACY!
ZEMO, GET AWAY FROM THE EDGE--
RMMBBLLEE
AAAAHHHH!
NO!
ZEMO!

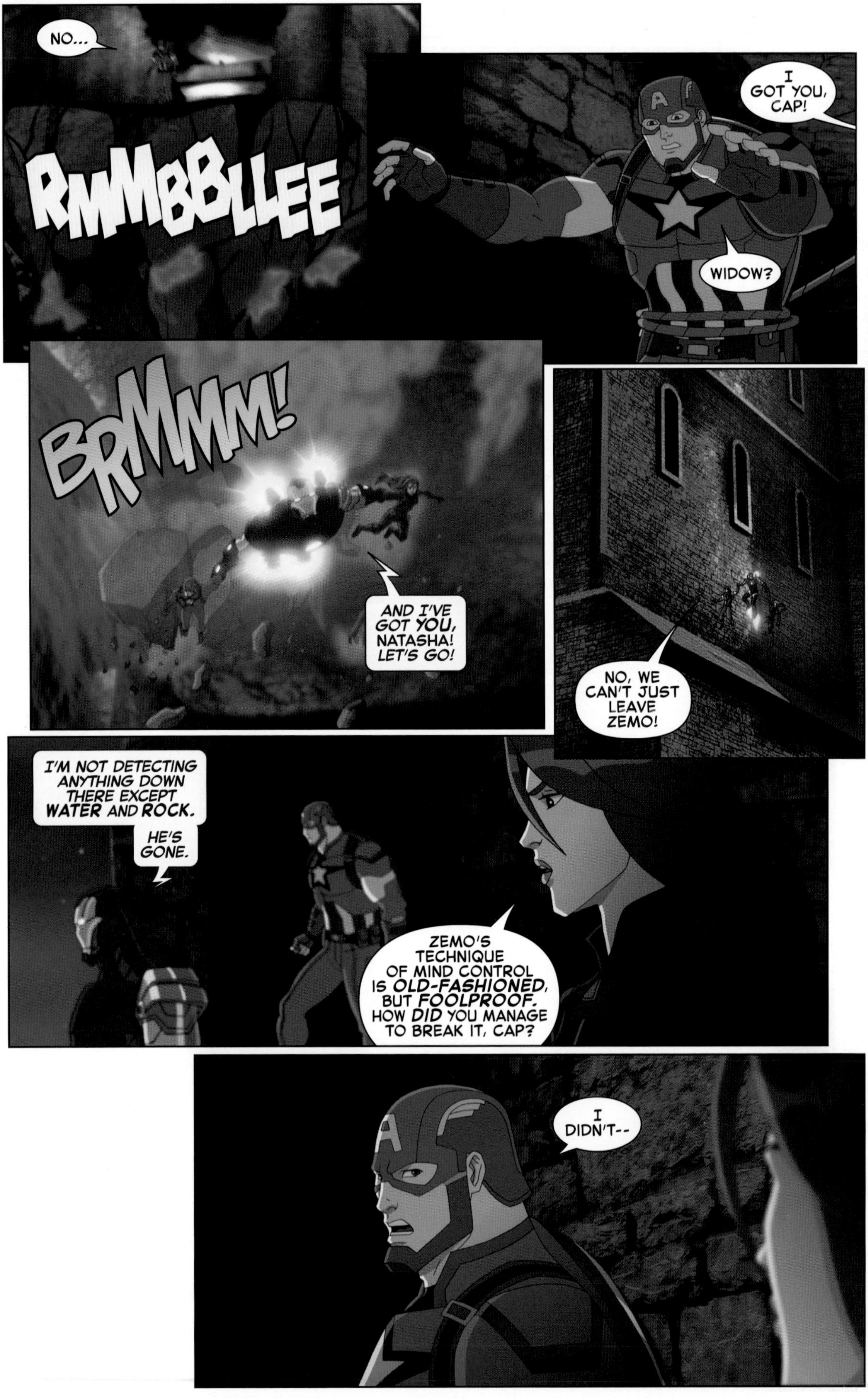
NO...
RMMBBLLEE
I GOT YOU, CAP!
WIDOW?
BRMMM!
AND I'VE GOT YOU, NATASHA! LET'S GO!
NO, WE CAN'T JUST LEAVE ZEMO!
I'M NOT DETECTING ANYTHING DOWN THERE EXCEPT WATER AND ROCK.
HE'S GONE.
ZEMO'S TECHNIQUE OF MIND CONTROL IS OLD-FASHIONED, BUT FOOLPROOF. HOW DID YOU MANAGE TO BREAK IT, CAP?
I DIDN'T--

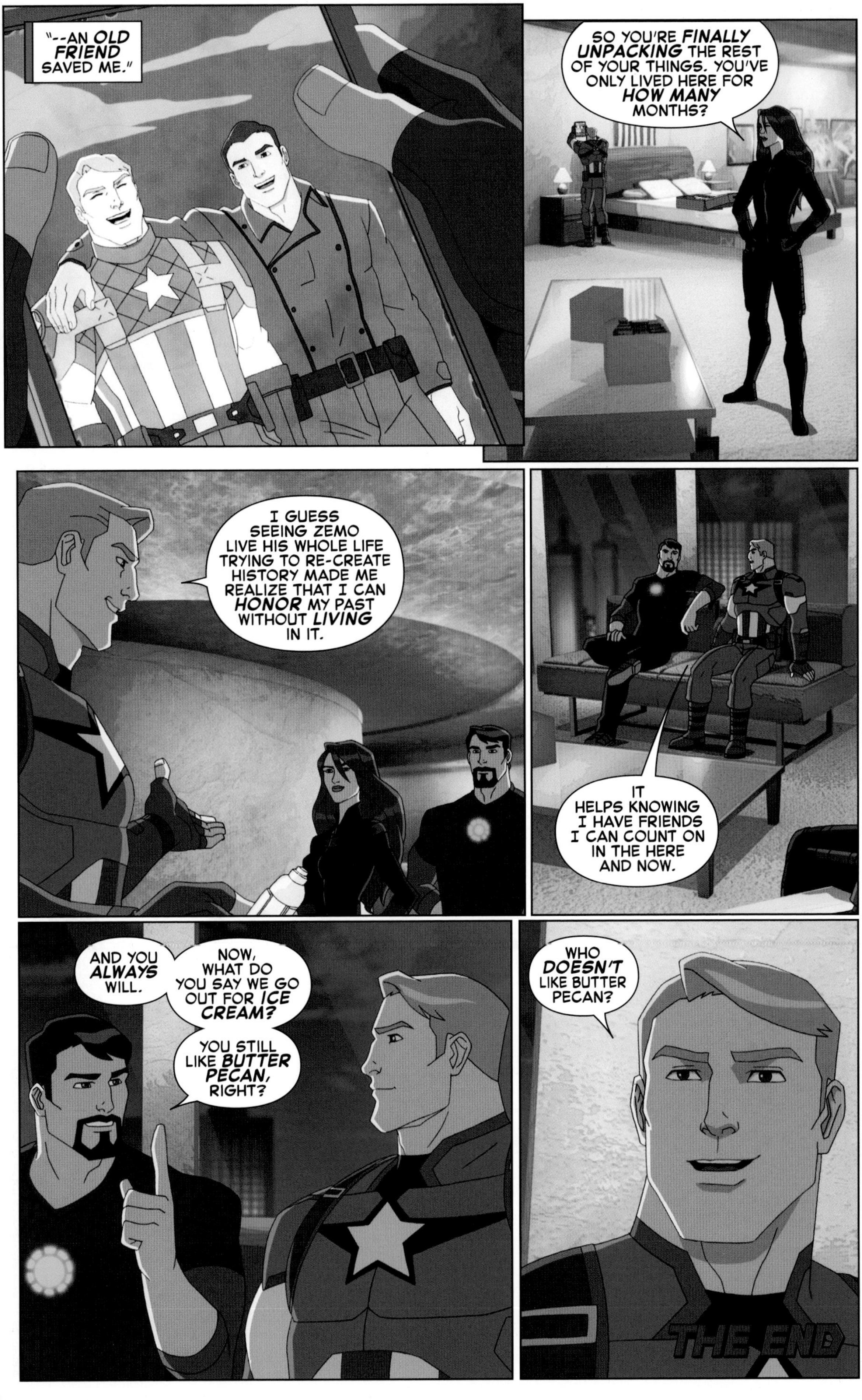
"--AN OLD FRIEND SAVED ME."
SO YOU'RE FINALLY UNPACKING THE REST OF YOUR THINGS. YOU'VE ONLY LIVED HERE FOR HOW MANY MONTHS?
I GUESS SEEING ZEMO LIVE HIS WHOLE LIFE TRYING TO RE-CREATE HISTORY MADE ME REALIZE THAT I CAN HONOR MY PAST WITHOUT LIVING IN IT.
IT HELPS KNOWING I HAVE FRIENDS I CAN COUNT ON IN THE HERE AND NOW.
AND YOU ALWAYS WILL.
NOW, WHAT DO YOU SAY WE GO OUT FOR ICE CREAM?
YOU STILL LIKE BUTTER PECAN, RIGHT?
WHO DOESN'T LIKE BUTTER PECAN?
THE END

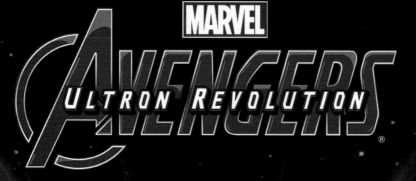

MARVEL

AVENGERS ULTRON REVOLUTION

COLLECT THEM ALL!

Set of 4 Hardcover Books ISBN: 978-1-5321-4345-8

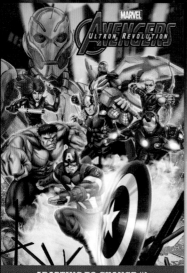

MARVEL
AVENGERS ULTRON REVOLUTION
ADAPTING TO CHANGE #1

Hardcover Book ISBN
978-1-5321-4346-5

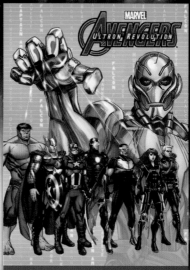

MARVEL
AVENGERS ULTRON REVOLUTION
THE ULTIMATES #2

Hardcover Book ISBN
978-1-5321-4347-2

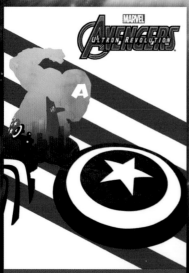

MARVEL
AVENGERS ULTRON REVOLUTION
SAVING CAPTAIN ROGERS #3

Hardcover Book ISBN
978-1-5321-4348-9

MARVEL
AVENGERS ULTRON REVOLUTION
DEHULKED #4

Hardcover Book ISBN
978-1-5321-4349-6

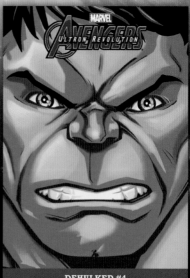